A SECRET IN TIME

SALLY NICHOLLS

nosy crow

First published in the UK in 2021 by Nosy Crow Ltd

The Crow's Nest, 14 Baden Place
Crosby Row, London, SE1 1YW

Nosy Crow and associated logos are trademarks and/or registered
trademarks of Nosy Crow Ltd.

ISBN: 978 0 85763 914 1

A CIP catalogue record for this book is available from the British Library.

Printed and bound in Great Britain by Clays Ltd, Elcograf S.p.A.

Papers used by Nosy Crow are made from wood grown in sustainable forests.

MIX
Paper from
responsible sources
FSC® C018072

3 5 7 9 10 8 6 4 2

www.nosycrow.com

CHAPTER ONE
THE FROZEN HOUSE

"It's hideous," said Ruby Pilgrim, staring at herself in the mirror. "Absolutely hideous. I look about eight! And you look even worse."

Alex didn't reply. Secretly he rather liked his new uniform. White shirt, grey shorts and blazer, red jersey and socks, striped tie. At his current school the uniform was a red sweatshirt and a T-shirt. At the big noisy school most of his friends were going to in September you wore a blue sweatshirt in winter, and a shirt and tie in summer. Alex didn't consider sweatshirts a proper uniform at all. This one looked *smart*.

"Seven maybe!" said Ruby in disgust. "Six!"

Things were, he had to admit, worse for Ruby. She was wearing what Aunt Joanna called a gymslip, but Alex and Ruby would have called a pinafore dress, the sort of thing only very little girls would ever have worn at their primary school. The striped tie and blazer were all right, but the whole thing looked most unRubyish. Ruby was

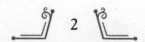

thirteen, and currently went to the secondary school with the blue sweatshirt. There she wore her tie as short as she could get away with, stuck badges all over the lapels of her coat and had pulled all the thread out of the school crest on her chest. There she looked like a teenager. Here she looked like something out of Enid Blyton.

"Everyone else will look the same," Alex said.

Ruby glared. "It's all right for you!" she said. "You'd have had to move schools anyway!"

It was true. Alex would be leaving primary school forever in September, and everything would change. The old, comfortable routine of glue sticks and topic books and school trays would be replaced with terrifying prospects like

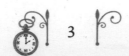

algebra and rugby and getting your head flushed down the toilets. He hadn't been looking forward to it *at all*.

But this new school…

Their parents had taken them on a tour. Ruby had been scowling and furious, but Alex was secretly thrilled. It had its own theatre. Its own swimming pool. Canoes and rowing boats that pupils took out on the river in PE. A beautiful old-fashioned library, with ladders on wheels. School trips to France to go skiing. ("Not that Mum and Dad could afford to send us on *those*!" said Ruby.)

"Only Aunt Joanna could think giving us money for *school* was a good idea," said Ruby. "St Caedmon's must cost thousands and *thousands* of

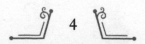

pounds. Just think what we could have done with that! We could go on a round-the-world cruise! We could buy our own yacht!"

"You don't even like boats!" said Alex. "And I don't think she's paying for *all* of it. Mum and Dad are helping."

He knew Aunt Joanna was trying to be kind. Last summer he and Ruby had stepped inside a magic time-travelling mirror and found themselves in 1912. There they'd helped save a Saxon treasure from some thieves and hidden it in a secret compartment in the sitting-room wall, where it had stayed until they'd triumphantly revealed it to Aunt Joanna. Aunt Joanna had sold the Newberry Cup at Christmas, and now she'd told their parents that she wanted them to have some of the money, as a thank-you. Only instead of just putting it in their bank accounts and letting them spend it on what they wanted, the money was to go towards this new, expensive school.

"Come on," he said. "Let's go and show Aunt Joanna the uniforms and get it over with."

Ruby pushed herself off the bed and went downstairs. Alex followed.

The big eighteenth-century mirror that had started all this hung in the hallway below the staircase. Alex glanced at it reflexively as he passed. Most of the time it just showed Aunt Joanna's hallway, with the front door and the tiled floor, and the little table with the guest book, and leaflets about local attractions. But sometimes…

"Ruby!"

Sometimes it didn't.

Sometimes it showed other reflections, long-ago hallways in long-ago Applecott Houses. And at those times you could step into it and be taken … well, who knew?

Somewhen else.

This time it showed a dark hallway, papered with dingy green paper, and what looked like a painting of a knight on a horse. A little girl was sitting on the floor laying out a train set. She looked about five or six, with fair hair and bright-blue eyes. Although she was inside she was wearing a brown coat, a pink woolly hat and scarf, and boots.

"All *right*," said Ruby. She looked at the reflection. "When do you think it is?"

Alex shrugged. It was hard to tell. Twentieth century definitely. Later than 1912, when the girls they'd met had worn petticoats and bodices and all sorts. But longer ago than the photographs of his parents' childhoods.

"Hey," Ruby said. "Do you think we should yell for Aunt Joanna? If she saw this, she'd *have* to believe us."

Alex felt a surge of panic. "No!" he said far too quickly. He was sure the mirror didn't want Aunt Joanna to know its secrets. "What if it closed? What if it never opened again? What if this is our *one chance*?"

"All right!" said Ruby. "It was just an idea." She caught hold of his sleeve. "Ready?" He nodded.

Ready.

And they stepped into the mirror.

The familiar sucking sensation. The familiar lurch in the pit of Alex's stomach. And the violence at the other end as they landed in a heap on the floor of the hallway at Applecott House. And – so sudden it felt like a physical attack – the cold.

It was freezing – literally, Alex realised, as he sat up and saw his breath coming out in icy clouds. Even in his new school jersey and blazer, it was desperately cold; midwinter, snowy-day-without-a-coat-on cold. The tiled hall floor against his hands and knees was almost colder than he could bear. He looked around, wondering if the door and windows were open or something, but, no, they were shut. It *was* snowing, though; through the windows he could see the thick white flakes falling through dusky twilight.

"Central heating!" moaned Ruby behind him. "Even the *Romans* had central heating! Please tell me they have some!"

But all Aunt Joanna's radiators had gone. Alex looked around him cautiously. The floor was patterned with the same black-and-white chessboard tiles it had had in 1912, but now they looked old and cracked and worn. There were several new pictures, and two stiff hard-backed chairs that hadn't been there before. The wallpaper was different, and so was the stair carpet, although it looked so tatty that it had obviously been there a long time. The whole hall looked worn and shabby and rather dingy. The front door was just the same as in 1912, though, with the same coloured glass in the fanlight. The hall table was the same, and the picture of the little girl with the cat, and, just as in the 1912 house, there was the faint background scent of tobacco. And, of course, the mirror was still there, in exactly the same place it had always hung in Aunt Joanna's hall.

The little girl sat surrounded by pieces of train set, her mouth open in amazement. Her cheeks were white with cold, Alex saw, and her hands were an awful blueish colour. There were raw red sores all over her fingers, like swollen scarlet blisters.

"Hello," said Alex. He gave her a little wave.

"Right," said Ruby. She dusted herself down. "Ruby Pilgrim. Alex Pilgrim. Time travellers from the twenty-first century, here to right wrongs and sort out stuff that needs sorting out and generally be awesome. You're probably related to us. What year is it, and what needs doing? And is it always this *cold*?"

The little girl gave them a sudden, completely unexpected smile, and shook her head. "It's the coldest winter in three hundred years," she said proudly. "It's 1947. Sillies! Fancy not knowing that! Have you come to help Colin find where the highwayman hid his treasure? How super!"

"I dunno," said Ruby. "Probably. Have you lost some highwayman's treasure?"

"No!" The little girl giggled. "It's Mrs Eddington's necklace Colin wants to find. It's—"

But she was interrupted by a noise behind her. It was the door to the living room opening to reveal two elderly women. One was pleasant-looking, with white hair and a pink scarf tied on to her head instead of a hat. Like the little girl, her nose was blue with cold and she was wearing her coat inside the house. Despite the cold, she gave the girl a quick smile and raised her eyebrows at Alex and Ruby.

"Hello! Where did you two spring from? I didn't miss the bell, did I? I must be going deaf in my old age. Oh!" Her face changed. "Oh, of course! You must be our evacuees from the hills! It'll be rather nice to have evacuees here again, won't it, Sheila? Quite like old times! Mrs Blackstaff *did*

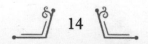

say she might billet some on us. That's right, isn't it?"

"Um," said Alex. "Yes?" The mirror was surprisingly good at providing them with a conveniently plausible-ish explanation for being wherever it was they'd landed this time. Maybe it was part of its magic? It was one advantage to hideously old-fashioned school uniforms at least. When you actually ended up somewhere hideously old-fashioned, you didn't stand out.

The other woman shook her head and pursed her lips. She looked older than the first lady. She was smaller and more wrinkled somehow, and her shoulders were hunched. She scowled at the children as though she thought the first lady was stupid for agreeing to house them.

As soon as she saw her, Sheila scrambled to her feet.

"Mrs Eddington!" she cried.

The cheerful-looking woman said, "Now, Sheila—"

But Sheila ignored her. "Mrs Eddington!" she said. "Daddy's coming home any day now – he is, isn't he, Granny?"

"Well, yes," said the cheerful woman, who must be Granny. "But, dear—"

"Mrs Eddington, *please* say you'll forgive him – *please*. If you don't—"

"Sheila!" said Granny.

Mrs Eddington's scowl grew deeper.

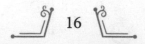

"But, Granny!" Sheila cried. "You always say we have to forgive people – like when I took Colin's magnifying glass and dropped it in the river by mistake; you said he had to forgive *me*!"

"Sheila, that's enough!"

Mrs Eddington held up her hand. She advanced on Sheila, her face hard and stony. "Your father," she said slowly, "is a liar and a thief. He is lucky I didn't report him to the constables, and if he comes begging at my door, I will certainly do so! Do you understand me?"

Sheila looked as though she were going to cry.

"He is not!" she said shrilly. "He isn't any of those things! And we're going to prove it!"

CHAPTER TWO
THE SECRET NECKLACE

"Well!" said Granny, as she shut the door behind Mrs Eddington. "*What* a welcome for our guests, I don't say! Really, Sheila!"

"But she shouldn't say those things!" said Sheila. "Daddy *isn't* a liar and a thief! He isn't!"

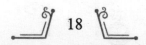

"Of course not," said Granny briskly. "But you'll never convince her, I'm afraid. Come now! She's a dreadful old woman, and let's not worry about her any more. Can you say hello to our evacuees, like a nice sensible child?"

"But they *aren't* evacuees," said Sheila, with a mulishness that was very like Ruby's. "They're time travellers! They've come to help Colin find Mrs Eddington's necklace!"

"That's enough silliness," said Granny. "They aren't anything of the kind! There's more snow expected tonight," she explained, looking fondly down at the child. "And it looks like some of the farms up on the hills are going to be snowed in. Mrs Blackstaff is trying to get people billeted on families in the village, and I said we'd take a couple of people in. Are we expecting your parents too, dear?"

"Um," said Alex again. "No, it's just us."

"Oh, of course!" the woman said. "They must be run off their feet. I don't think we've met, dear. I'm Mrs Pilgrim. I'm Sheila's granny." She smiled down at the little girl. "Colin and Janet should be around somewhere – the whole brood were evacuated here during the war, and since it's taking *such* an age to demob the men, we're lucky enough to still have them. But Daddy should be home any day now, shouldn't he, darling?"

"Dad's in Japan," said Sheila proudly.

Alex guessed he must be in the army or navy or

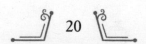

something – everyone was in the Second World War, weren't they? He wondered what "demob" meant. A mob was a big gang of people, like an army was, so maybe it meant break up a mob and send everyone home. He knew the Second World War was between 1939 and 1945 (there was a big display all about it on the corridor wall opposite his classroom). He'd thought all the soldiers had just came home when it ended, but perhaps they hadn't.

"Ruby and Alex," said Ruby. "Er, Jones. Ruby Jones."

"Lovely!" said Granny. "Now, where are your bags, dears? I'll take them up and show you your rooms. And I must tell Mrs Culpepper we've two more for dinner. Oh! And could you let me have your ration books before I forget?"

Alex and Ruby exchanged a panicked glance. Ration books. Alex knew all about them – lots of food was rationed in the war, like bread and meat and butter, and you had to hand over ration coupons to get them. He wasn't sure why you'd still need them in 1947, two years after the war had ended, but apparently you did. What was going to happen when they didn't hand one over? Would they starve?

"We, um, we don't have them," he said. He looked at Granny and saw, quite distinctly, the expression on her face. It was one of real horror.

"There, um, there was an – an accident, when

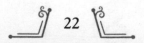

we were, er, coming down the hill," said Ruby. "Our bags were lost!"

"Lost?"

"Yeah, they, um, they fell off the back of my dad's truck. And our ration books were in them. My dad was going to look out for them on the way back up, but it's been snowing, and it's dark, and – well. He said he'd try to bring them back down again if he found them, but I don't know if he's going to be able to make it through the snow."

She looked anxiously at Granny to see how she would take this story, which Alex thought sounded pretty implausible. Granny drew in her breath. Alex thought she was going to be angry, but instead she said rather shakily, "Oh, well!

Worse things happen at sea, I suppose. I'll have a talk with Mrs Blackstaff and see if she can send some coupons our way. And we'll get on with sorting you out a replacement. Now—"

Alex and Ruby gave each other a nervous glance. Alex wasn't sure how you replaced a lost ration book, but he was pretty sure there wouldn't be an Alex and Ruby Jones on any official list. And what was going to happen when Granny rang Mrs Blackstaff and asked them to help with those children she'd supposedly sent to Applecott House?

Granny, meanwhile, was looking about her anxiously. "I think, dears," she was saying, "I might get Colin and Janet to show you to the spare

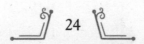

room, then I can go and talk to Mrs Culpepper and see what we've got in for dinner. Colin!" she called up the stairs. "Janet! Can you come down here a minute! It's *such* a bother the phone lines being down in the snow. But I'm sure I'll be able to get through to Mrs Blackstaff tomorrow."

So they had a day at least. That was something.

There was a clatter on the stairs and a boy and a girl appeared on the landing. Alex supposed they must be Sheila's brother and sister. The boy, Colin, looked about thirteen, with thick fair hair and round glasses. He was wearing a green knitted jersey, grey flannel shorts (shorts! In this weather! Even Alex's new posh school only expected you to wear shorts in warm weather) and grey knitted knee socks. *Just William*, thought Alex, and grinned to himself. On top of this he wore an overcoat and a blue bobble hat that, rather unexpectedly, looked almost identical to a hat Alex's granny had knitted for him when he was little. The girl, who must be Janet, was wearing a dark-blue knitted jersey, a thick green knee-length skirt and black knitted stockings. Janet also wore a woolly hat and a coat that looked for all the world like it had been made out of a blanket. She had brown hair, which she wore in a neat bob kept back with a black hair slide. She had a pinched little face with an anxious expression, and she looked about eleven.

"There you are!" Granny was saying cheerfully. "This great boy is my grandson Colin, and this

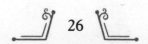

little love is Janet. This is Ruby and Alex. They're from one of the farms on the hill, and we're taking them in until the snow's over. They've lost all their bags, so can you show them where the guest rooms are and find them something a bit warmer to wear? I'm sorry this house is so perishing," she added, turning to them. "Old houses always are, aren't they? Give me a good old-fashioned farmhouse kitchen any day. And with all the coal shortages... We do what we can, but if you feel like you're about to catch pneumonia, do give me a shout."

Alex was beginning to think pneumonia was a serious possibility. His hands were going a curious shade of blue, and his feet felt rather like blocks of ice. Ruby had stuck her hands under her armpits, but her nose was a raw, painful-looking red, and so were her ears. Perhaps there would be some old coats tucked away in a drawer somewhere. Although… Alex looked doubtfully at Janet's blanket coat. It didn't seem very likely. He smiled at Colin and Janet hopefully. Janet gave him a shy smile back and Colin waggled his ears and grinned.

"C'mon then," he said. "Golly! Don't you have *any* luggage at all?"

He led them up the stairs, talking cheerfully over his shoulder.

"I say! Are your parents going to be snowed in then? How wizard! Janet and I *long* to be snowed in. Did you have to dig your way out like Eskimos?

I bet you wish they'd left you up there to live off wild animals and melted snow, don't you? I suppose they thought you couldn't interrupt your educations – grown-ups are always fussing about people's mouldy old educations. What schools *do* you go to anyway? The village school doesn't have a uniform. And you don't go to the Grammar, or we'd know you."

"Um," said Alex. "It's St Caedmon's. It's, um, a boarding school. But. Um. We aren't there at the moment because of, um, mumps."

Being sent home from school because of mumps had happened to someone in a book he'd read once. As soon as he'd said it, he realised what a stupid explanation it was – if they'd been sent home from school, why would they still be in school uniform? And why would they need to be evacuated? But Colin seemed to accept it easily enough.

"Well, there you are," he said, flinging open the bedroom door. "Beds. Windows. Wardrobe. All the usual domestic conveniences."

It was a big and rather bare room (in Aunt Joanna's Applecott House it had been chopped into two smaller bed and breakfast rooms and a bathroom), with two severe-looking single bedsteads and the usual eiderdown-blanket-sheet affair.

"I'll just open the window," said Janet, hurrying over to the sash.

Ruby squawked. "Are you *mad*? It's *freezing*!

What do you want to open the *window* for?"

Janet looked hurt. "Oh, but fresh air is frightfully important—" she began.

"Oh, dry up!" cried Sheila, who had been waiting with increasing impatience for the formal part of the showing-around to be over. "They aren't from the hills at all! They're from the future! They've come to help us find Mrs Eddington's necklace!"

There was a short, rather stunned pause. Then Janet said, "Sheila, you *mustn't* tell stories."

"I wasn't telling stories!"

"*And*," said Colin crushingly, "I don't know that people of six have any right to go telling *our* family secrets to strangers—"

"She didn't tell us anything really," said Alex

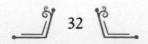

hastily. "She just said you might want some help—"

Behind Colin, Ruby mouthed *Shut up, Sheila!* and made frantic "shut up" gestures with her hands.

"And it isn't as though it's a secret exactly," Janet said. "Everyone in the village knows all about it."

"Oh, the village!" said Colin scornfully.

"And so it's my family secret just as much as yours!" said Sheila indignantly. "And they said they were going to *help* us! Only I 'spect they won't bother now you're being so *putrid*, and Daddy will have to live with the shame forever, and we'll have to go away – and—"

Her little face was red with fury. Colin gave

Alex a helpless glance that said *Sisters!* as clearly as though he'd spoken.

Janet said, "Oh, Sheila, *do* stop it, *please.*" She looked anxiously at Colin, and said, "They may as *well* help since they're here. I mean, it would be pretty beastly to leave them out. It's not *their* fault Sheila's such a little ass."

Colin hesitated. Then he sighed. "Oh, all *right*," he said. "But you can't tell a *soul* – cross your heart and hope to die."

Ruby said, "Yes, yes, anything you like. Swear on Alex's life. As long as we can have some coats or something before we all die of frostbite?"

"Yes, why don't you have coats?" said Colin. "We're far too polite to ask, but we did wonder."

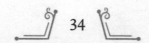

"Lost our luggage," said Ruby briefly. "And there are rugs and things in Dad's truck, so we didn't need them. Why are you wearing *shorts* in winter?"

"Isn't Alex wearing shorts?" said Janet, surprised, looking at Alex's school uniform.

"Only for school," said Alex awkwardly. "Normally I wear trousers. Don't—"

But he was interrupted by a loud *gong*ing noise from downstairs.

Sheila cried, "Oh, dinner! Good-oh."

Alex felt a strange sinking sensation in his stomach. Food. Ration books. Would there even be anything for them to eat?

CHAPTER THREE
MAKE DO
AND MEND

They charged down the stairs. Alex was wearing
a grown-out-of coat that had once belonged to
Colin, so worn that the elbows were shiny with
wear, and the collar was almost frayed away. Ruby
was in a man's leather coat, which apparently

belonged to the children's father, a woollen scarf and a man's winter hat. Alex secretly thought she looked rather glamorous.

They burst into the dining room, which looked like a shabbier, more tired version of its 1912 self. The paint on the skirting boards and the window frames was chipped and grimy. There were scuff marks on the wallpaper and soot stains over the fireplace that nobody had bothered to clean. The rug looked so worn there were actually bare threads where the weave had been rubbed away. Threadbare, literally.

Sitting at the head of the table was an old man scowling at his plate. He looked tired too. Tired and cold and grumpy. The whole of Applecott

House looked tired. Alex supposed world wars *must* be tiring. He wondered if they still had servants. 1912 Applecott House had had a maid and a cook and two men to do the gardening and the rough work. Here there just seemed to be Mrs Culpepper, a big, rather elderly woman, who shuffled in with the plates of food then shuffled out again. At school they just talked about evacuees and bomb shelters and spitfires and ration books. They didn't talk about everything looking tired and dirty and not having enough food.

"Grandfather!" Sheila cried as they came in. "Look who's come to stay with us!"

Grandfather looked up and grunted. "So!" he said. "You're the young limbs who want to turn

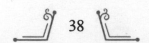

up and eat all our rations, are you? Didn't anyone tell you, if you're going to lose your ration book you should at least have the decency to do it in your own house!"

"Dear!" said Granny. "It isn't the children's fault."

"We're very sorry," Alex said hastily. "And we're very grateful to you for letting us stay at all."

Grandfather grunted. "Huh!"

They sat down at the table and looked around. Food was one of Alex's favourite things about the past. Blancmange, and tea (an extra meal in between lunch and supper that mostly consisted of cake), and home-grown fruit and vegetables, and eggs and ham from nearby farms. Food from the past was generally simpler than food in the present – no pizza or takeaway or Haribo – but in Applecott House at any rate it had all tasted *good*.

This dinner was just depressing. There was a serving dish full of potatoes, another full of carrots and turnips and cabbage, and plates with slices of pink wobbly-looking fried meat. There

was plenty of vegetables, but the portions of meat were tiny. Alex thought it very likely that his and Ruby's portions had been taken from everyone else's.

"Is this all there *is*?" said Sheila loudly.

Janet said, "Hush!" with an anxious glance in their direction.

Sheila wailed, "But I'm *hungry*!"

Alex felt an awful squirmy guilty feeling in his stomach. They were eating these people's food. They obviously didn't have much, and he and Ruby were eating it.

He swallowed and said, "It's all right. I mean, I'm not very hungry." He could feel Ruby glaring at him. Actually, he felt much more hungry than usual, perhaps because it was so cold.

"Oh, for pity's sake!" It was Granny. "Nobody is going hungry in this house. Do you hear me? You are our guests, and you will be fed. I'll talk to Mrs Blackstaff at church tomorrow and see if she can help, and hopefully on Monday the roads will still be clear enough to get into Felixstowe and get you new ration books. Do your parents usually shop in the village, do you know? We might persuade Mr Harrow to advance us something, if he knows who you are."

"Er –" Alex shot a panicked look at Ruby – "er, no, no, I don't think so. Mum goes, er…" He trailed off. Their cover story was suddenly beginning to look a lot less clever. What was going to happen when Granny talked to Mrs Blackstaff and realised that she had no idea who they were? How were they possibly going to explain themselves?

"And as for you!" This was directed at Sheila. "I've never been so ashamed of a child in my life. When we have guests in our house, we eat the food on our plates and we are *thankful* for it. Do I make myself clear?"

She did. And her tone was so awful it even shut Ruby up. She ate the pink meat, which turned out to be Spam and tasted disgusting. She pulled the most awful face when she did so, but she swallowed it down and even managed to say "Thank you very much, that was lovely" when she was done. At least it was warm. Alex could feel it warming him up from the inside out.

"Lovely!" said Granny with an amused expression. "My dear child, it was perfectly revolting, and don't you pretend any different."

"Ruddy Labour government!" Grandfather muttered. "Rationing our bread to pay for their National Health Service – what a ridiculous idea

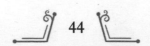

that was! Don't know what the country's coming to!"

"I don't think the bread shortage has anything to do with the National Health Service, darling," said Granny comfortingly.

"I say, Granny," Colin said. "Alex says he wears long trousers – and he's younger than I am! May *I* wear long trousers too?"

"Long trousers!" Granny gave Alex a look of combined amusement and disapproval. "I pity whoever has the darning of *your* knees. Go through them as soon as blinking, most boys would."

The children all looked at the spot where Alex's knees presumably were, underneath the table and the empty plate.

Alex squirmed. He didn't think anyone had ever darned them in his life. "Well…" he said. "They don't really need darning. I mean … you grow out of them before they do usually. Or I do anyway."

"Indeed. And how long would a pair of long trousers last you then?"

"Um…" Alex glanced at Ruby. He'd never paid much attention to how long clothes lasted. "I dunno. A year? Six months?"

"Six months!" Granny laughed. "Oh, to live in such a land of plenty! I suppose clothes rations grow on trees in your house, do they?"

"Golly!" Colin said. "I've had these shorts two and a half years. Granny kept letting them down, only now she's run out of hem so they're just

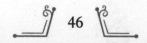

getting shorter."

"Do you really get a whole new outfit every six months?" said Janet.

"*An* outfit?" Ruby stared. "How many changes of clothes do you *have*?"

"Well..." Janet considered. "School uniform. Two winter skirts and two pairs of shorts for summer. Two shirts. Two jerseys – and my school cardigan, of course. Two vests. Stockings."

"And knickers!" said Sheila. "Three pairs of knickers! And a party frock – only mine used to be Janet's and it's *quite* the wrong shape, so it *bulges* in the most peculiar places. You *are* lucky, just having a sister," she said to Alex.

Ruby's face was a picture of horror. "*Three* pairs

of knickers! How often do you change them?"

"Every week." Janet looked surprised. "How often do you?"

"Every *day*," said Ruby. "That's *disgusting*. And you've only got one change of clothes! I've got *loads* more clothes than that. And *vests*! Yuck! That's such an old-man thing to wear."

"That's enough," said Granny firmly. "Some of us are trying to eat, not talk about underwear at the dinner table."

Janet had gone pink. She looked as though she might be about to cry.

"I wish we had vests," Alex said quickly. "*And* I wish we had proper woolly jumpers like yours – I'm freezing in these!"

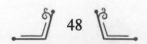

"I bet you jolly well are," Janet said. No, she wasn't upset; she was angry. "I wouldn't want heaps of clothes anyway! You sound horribly spoilt. And affected!"

"*Janet!*"

"Well, she *does*."

"I don't even know what that *means*," Ruby muttered, but she kept her mouth shut throughout pudding, which was a white gloopy mess with balls of what looked like frogspawn in it. It was apparently called tapioca and it tasted marginally less disgusting than it looked but only just. It was served with stewed apples from the garden, which tasted just like Aunt Joanna's stewed apples, only with less sugar.

In between mouthfuls Alex stole glances at Colin and Janet and Sheila. All their clothes had a rather worn and faded look about them. Janet's jersey had been darned in several places, with wool that was almost – but not exactly – the same colour. Sheila's skirt had a decidedly home-made look about it, and there was something about the way the cloth had worn that made Alex wonder if it had been cut down from a larger skirt belonging to somebody else. There was a darker stripe at the bottom where a hem had obviously been let down to make it longer. Even Colin's *coat* was darned.

Alex hadn't worn hand-me-downs since he was a toddler. All his clothes came new from a shop. You didn't darn the knees or turn down the hems

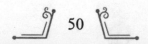

when you tore clothes or grew out of them. You just went and bought new ones.

Except in 1947, you didn't.

When dinner was over, Grandfather and Granny went into the living room, where there was a large wood fire burning. Alex had supposed that they'd go too – fire! Actual fire! Heat! – but Colin shook his head.

"Come up to HQ where we can talk properly," he said. And, as Ruby opened her mouth to argue, he added, "It's warm. I promise."

HQ, which stood for headquarters, was a large wooden cupboard on the top-floor landing. Inside was an old-fashioned-looking boiler surrounded by long slatted wooden shelves, with sheets and blankets and pillowcases and so forth piled on top of them. The pipes coming out of the top of the cupboard had been wrapped in blankets – "So they don't freeze," Sheila said casually, as though pipes freezing *indoors* was completely normal – but inside the cupboard—

"Heat!" said Ruby. "Oh, heat! Blessed heat!"

They crawled on to the shelves. Ruby wrapped herself in a blanket and rested her back against the boiler. "Oh God, this is the best thing *ever*," she said. "You guys can find the necklace. I am *never* leaving."

Colin shut the cupboard door and turned on a torch. The atmosphere felt suddenly

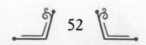

conspiratorial, like playing at pirates. For the first time Alex felt like they belonged.

"Well," Colin said, "Janet's right that it isn't exactly a secret – but it's hardly something we want talked about in the village. It all happened so long ago that mostly people don't talk about it any more – and we'd like to keep it like that."

"Not that Dad did anything wrong exactly – well, not *very* wrong," said Janet hastily. "It's just – well, *you* know."

"Our lips are sealed," said Ruby. "Now, spill."

CHAPTER FOUR
THE HIGHWAYMAN'S GOLD

"Well," said Colin, "Jan and I were evacuated here in 1939."

"On a train with labels round your neck?" said Ruby.

"No," said Colin. He sounded surprised.

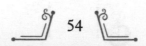

"Mum just telephoned Granny and Grandfather and asked if we could live with them," Janet explained.

"We all came – Mum and Dad as well. Dad got a job as a steward on Mrs Eddington's estate. Mrs Eddington lives in Oakden House, you know," Colin added.

The children nodded. They did know. Oakden was the big house on the edge of the village.

"Dad wanted to join the navy," Colin went on, "but he'd had TB, so they said he'd have to wait until he was fit. He joined up after Sheila was born."

"And he hasn't come home yet?" said Alex. This had been puzzling him. "But the war's over now, isn't it?"

"Yes, but Granny says they couldn't bring all the men home at once; it would be a frightful muddle. And then – well – Mum died when Sheila was little. So we're still here."

"Wow," said Ruby.

Alex agreed. Imagine your dad going off to Japan for years and years, and then your mum dying! It wouldn't matter how nice your grandparents were; it couldn't have been anything but awful.

"*Anyway*," Colin said hurriedly, as though he didn't want to talk about that, "we'd not been living here long when we found out about the highwayman's treasure."

Alex was sharing a shelf with Colin. He could see, therefore, the rather solemn, almost religious expression that crossed his face.

"*I've fallen for you,*" he said, "*little apple-dweller.*" He sounded as though he were reciting poetry. "*They cannot force us apart. I'll keep your secret hidden.*"

There was a pause.

"You *what?*" said Ruby. "What does that even *mean?*"

Colin grinned. "It's an old story," he said. "Apparently there used to be this highwayman who was in love with a girl who lived at Applecott House, ages ago, back in the days of highwaymen. He made his fortune robbing people on the roads, and the story was he and the girl were going to elope. Her parents didn't want her to marry a highwayman, naturally. But on the night they were supposed to run away together there was a blizzard, and while he was fighting his way through the snow on his horse he was arrested. And then he was tried for theft and hanged. They kept asking him where all his gold was hidden, but he wouldn't tell them. But on the scaffold he looked at the girl he loved, who was standing there watching him go, you know, and he said that riddle to her."

"But what does it *mean*?" said Ruby.

"It's where his treasure was hidden, of course," said Janet. "You juggins. Everyone kept asking the

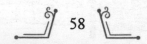

girl where it was. But she wouldn't tell them. And she always said she *couldn't* get it. Not that she didn't know where it was – just that she couldn't get it."

"Is that *real*?" said Ruby sceptically.

"Oh yes," said Janet. "There's a display about it in the museum in town and everything. I know it sounds like rot, but it's real enough."

"And nobody ever found the treasure?" said Alex.

The children all started talking at once.

"They did!" cried Sheila.

"That's what this whole thing is about!" said Janet.

"Oh yes," said Colin. He looked rather grim.

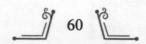

"That's where all our problems begin."

"Tell it in the proper order," Ruby begged.

"Well," Janet said, "Mum loved that story when she was a kid. She and her brothers always used to say they were going to solve the riddle, and they used to go looking for the treasure, but they never found it. When Mum told us the story, she always said she thought she knew where it was, but she'd never say where.

"'If I'm right, it's not going anywhere any time soon,' she used to say. 'And I'm not having you lot going after it and breaking your necks!'"

"But didn't she want to find it herself?" Ruby said, puzzled.

"We used to ask her that," Colin said. "But she'd

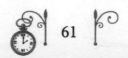

just say she *couldn't*. Just like the girl, you see?"

"Hmm." Ruby sounded doubtful.

"*Anyway*," Janet said, "she never did do anything about it until the winter Dad went off to join the navy. It was New Year's Eve, and Mum and Dad were going to a dance at the barracks at Stowe Cottley. They hadn't been to a party for simply years, only with Dad going away, you know, they wanted one last night before they had to say goodbye. So Dad took an old dress from Mrs Eddington's wardrobe. I know he shouldn't have, but he was going to take it back the next day, and Mrs Eddington wouldn't have known any better. It was about a million years old, he said; it wasn't like she was going to miss it. And he took her handbag too. The dress was beautiful, Granny says – all sort of floaty, with simply acres of silk, very loose. And in the handbag there was this small, old silver locket that just looked perfect with it. It was a dreadfully cold night, all icy and everything frozen, and Dad always said Mum looked like the Snow Queen."

"But then she spilt red wine down it and everything was ruined?" said Ruby.

Janet shook her head. "The next day everything was still all frozen, and there was snow everywhere. And suddenly Mum got ever so excited, Dad said. She kept insisting they had to go and find the highwayman's treasure. That she thought she knew where it was and this was their one chance to find it before Dad had to leave."

"But why?" Alex said. "What had changed?"

"Dad didn't say," Colin said. "But Jan and I have an idea. Anyway, Dad wouldn't go. He said she was loopy, that the highwayman's riddle was just a kids' story, and he had far too much to do getting ready to go off. Dad's super – he really is – but, well…"

"It's all right," said Ruby. "We've got grown-ups of our own. We know."

"So then he and Mum had this awful row, and Mum said she was going to go anyway. She stormed off, and he stomped off to get on with packing – for the navy, you know. He thought – well, I don't know what he thought. But Mum—"

"Mum found the treasure!" Sheila said. She gave a little bounce, rattling the slats of the cupboard shelves.

"Not really?" said Ruby.

"Really, honestly, truly," said Colin. "Here, I'd better come out so you can see properly."

He opened the door to the cupboard and pushed himself out. The cold air was like opening a freezer door; Alex shivered. He was beginning to think Ruby might be right; maybe they could just spend all this adventure sitting here in the warm. Colin fumbled in his pocket and pulled out an old, battered-looking jewellery case, of the sort people put engagement rings in on telly. Alex and Ruby leant forward, watching as he took off the lid.

There, resting on what looked like cotton wool, was a heavy gold signet ring and a small pile of thin, old-looking golden coins. They glowed with a dull golden shine that was surprisingly vivid in the shabby room."Real gold!" said Ruby.

Janet looked at her in surprise and said, "Of course. Haven't you ever seen a sovereign before?"

"It's the highwayman's treasure!" said Sheila, bouncing on the slats again. "Well, some of it anyway! Mum found simply *piles* of it, but she couldn't bring it all back – just what she could put in her pockets and that necklace round her neck because it was so beautiful."

"Grandfather got it valued," said Colin. "It's highwayman's treasure all right – well, it's the right age anyway."

"But where was it?" Ruby asked.

Janet shook her head. "We don't know," she said sadly. "Mum—" She faltered.

"Mum caught hypothermia," said Colin flatly. "Being out in the snow, you know. Granny put her straight to bed when she got back, and called the doctor, but the telephone lines were down, and it took simply an age to find him. And then she died anyway. So."

Alex and Ruby were silent. What could you possibly say to that?

"I'm sorry," said Ruby awkwardly. "I mean—"

"Yes, it was rather beastly," said Colin briskly.

Alex was shocked. Perhaps this was the stiff

upper lip English people were supposed to have?

"But we can't do anything about that now," Colin continued.

"That wasn't the only thing that happened," Janet explained. "You see, the next morning, when everyone was so worried about Mum, Mrs Eddington came round in an awful temper, calling Dad a thief and all the names under the sun. Someone had seen Mum at the dance, you see, and told her about it and she was furious. Dad tried to explain that he'd just borrowed the things, but she wouldn't listen. She demanded he give them back *right then* – so he did. Or he tried to. But when he went into Mum's room, the dress and the bag were still there, but the necklace was gone."

"Someone had stolen it?"

Janet looked shocked. "Oh no! Mum was still wearing it when she went after the treasure. Dad distinctly remembered. And then when she came back she was wearing the highwayman's necklace – that one in Colin's box there. She must have taken off the locket to try the new necklace on and forgotten to bring it back with her. Dad did try to explain, but Mrs Eddington wouldn't listen. She was *furious*. She went completely potty, Dad says. She said he must have stolen it and sold it."

"As if Daddy ever would!" added Sheila.

"Of course he wouldn't," said Janet. "He'd only borrowed it. But that's what she said. She told

Dad that if he wasn't going off to join the navy, she'd have sacked him on the spot, and if he ever wanted to work for her again, he'd jolly well have to find her locket and give it back to her."

"But does he want to work for her again?" Alex asked.

"Of course he does!" cried Sheila.

"He needs to do something!" said Colin. "And besides…"

"If he can't get a job with Mrs Eddington, he'll have to go somewhere else." said Janet. "We'll have to leave – well, everything. Applecott House…"

"School," said Colin. "I mean, school's pretty putrid, of course, but I've just got into the upper third, and that's when you start playing rugger.

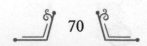

They said I'd probably be on the team if I kept it up like this, and Jan's a form prefect this year, which is a pretty feeble thing to care about, but you know girls –" Ruby snorted – "and there's the Scouts – we're going to climb Snowdon in the summer; it would be beastly to miss that—"

"And Peggy and Mary and Susan and Joan – I can't leave *them* behind!" cried Sheila.

"And Granny and Grandfather," said Janet. "They don't *say* they mind, of course, but…"

But they're basically our parents. Janet didn't say it, but she didn't need to. It hung there unsaid. Alex wondered how much of her father Sheila had actually seen. It couldn't be much, if he'd been in the navy since she was a baby.

"And besides," Janet said, going pink, "to have people – people thinking he was, you know, a *thief*..."

"It isn't to be borne," said Colin firmly. "Family honour and all that."

"All right," Ruby said. "I mean, we'll try, of course. But do you have *any* idea what that riddle was on about? Cos I don't."

"Well..." said Janet. "Colin thought..."

Colin cleared his throat, suddenly shy. "Well ..." he said, "1836 was cold, wasn't it? So I was wondering – what if it's only something that works when it's really cold? Like – what if it's hidden on an island you can only get to when it's frozen or something? The girl didn't say she

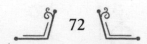

didn't know where it was; she said she *couldn't* get it. So it must be something it needs to be really, *really* cold for. I mean, it might be. That's what I thought. And the year Mum died was really cold too; Granny always said so. That's why the doctor took so long to come, because of the snow. Why else would she just rush off on the day Dad was leaving and everything?

"*And*," said Janet excitedly, "1947 is the coldest winter in three hundred years! They said so on the wireless."

"And that's why we have to find it *now*," said Colin. "Because if we wait until Dad gets home, the cold might have gone, and we might not get another chance for another hundred years! We solve the riddle, find the treasure and everything will be all right. Simple!"

Alex looked at Ruby. She nodded grimly. Today was Saturday. On Sunday Granny was going to talk to Mrs Blackstaff, the woman who had supposedly evacuated them to her house. Even if they could think of a way to stop that happening, on Monday she was going to go into town to find replacement ration cards for two children called Ruby and Alex Jones.

If they were going to solve this riddle, they were going to have to do it fast.

CHAPTER FIVE
QUESTIONS

They spent several minutes going round in circles over the riddle until Sheila started howling in frustration and boredom, and insisted they went downstairs to "Play *games*! Or *something*! *Anything* but this!"

Downstairs in the living room Grandfather was smoking a pipe and reading an old-fashioned-looking book and Granny was darning stockings. There was a big fire in the grate, and round the hearth it was wonderfully, blessedly warm.

They collapsed on the hearthrug and played several noisy rounds of old maid and snap, until Granny announced it was Sheila's bedtime and dragged her, complaining, upstairs. Then they played whist and rummy and a game Ruby said she had played at school with a very rude name that she had to whisper so Grandfather wouldn't hear.

Janet looked shocked, and Colin thought it was hilarious. And then Granny said, "Bedtime!" And

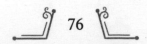

that was that.

Alex and Ruby, of course, had not brought pyjamas.

"But it's fine really," said Ruby. "If you think I'm *undressing*, you've got about fifty million other thinks coming."

Ruby, however, had reckoned without Granny. Alex was presented with a pair of Colin's outgrown pyjamas, which had actual blue-and-white stripes, like something out a picture book. They were made of flannel, and were a lot thicker than Alex's pyjamas at home. Ruby was given a pair that had apparently once belonged to the children's mother. Presumably they'd been kept until Janet was old enough to grow into them, which was a rather horrifying thought.

"And you might want these," Granny added grimly, throwing them a balaclava and an extra blanket each. "I'm afraid the guest room gets rather chilly in winter."

She wasn't kidding.

"Victorian times weren't this cold, were they?" said Alex.

"Victorians didn't wear shorts in midwinter!" said Ruby. "Remember? We had layers and layers of petticoats and stomachers and shawls and things. I'm going to put my jumper on! And I'm *definitely* going to shut the window."

It took what felt like forever to get to sleep. But

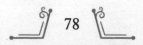

the morning was – if anything – even worse. Some sort of magic had happened overnight to the bed, which was now so warm it felt luxurious, like a hot bath or a sauna. The air outside the covers, in contrast, was actually *icy*.

"I am *never* getting up," said Ruby. "Never. Never! They cannot *possibly* expect me to take off my clothes in this weather."

Granny also took a very dim view of this.

"Come on!" she said briskly. "Breakfast in twenty minutes! Up! Up! Oh, and the pipes have frozen again, so it's the outside lav, I'm afraid, and you'll have to wash in the kitchen – luckily we've got the pump in the stable yard, otherwise I don't know *what* we'd do."

"You might as well do as she says," Sheila said, appearing in the doorway. "Or she'll come and strip the bedclothes off, and you'll have to get dressed in the cold." She sat on the end of Alex's bed. "Don't you have winters in the future?"

"We have central heating," said Alex. "And climate change." He was looking again at the red sores on Sheila's fingers. Chilblains. Everyone had had them in Victorian Applecott House too, but they still worried him.

"And look," said Ruby, "you've got to *promise* not to tell anyone about us coming from the future, OK? It's just going to make things complicated, and grown-ups never believe us anyway. We've tried and tried telling our mum and dad and they just think we're playing a game."

"Promise!" said Sheila, sitting up like a little dog. "Our secret – how super!"

"And we *can't* let your granny talk to Mrs Blackstaff or our cover will be blown," Alex added. "We'll have to stop her going to church."

"Stop Granny going to church?" said Sheila. "Golly! How are you going to do that?"

"How should I know?" said Ruby crossly. "But we'll have to think of something."

They dressed under the covers and put on their coats. The early-morning house was terrifyingly cold. And—

"Look!" said Ruby.

The bedroom windows were covered in feathery

fern-leaf patterns of frost – no, not frost, ice! Actual ice!

"Jack Frost," said Sheila, following her finger. "Doesn't he draw on your windows where you come from?"

"No," said Ruby. "Our houses aren't so cold you have *ice* on them! Is that *normal*?"

"I think so," said Sheila. "Golly, aren't houses cold at all in the future? You *are* lucky."

Alex supposed they were.

"They're beautiful, though," he said wistfully, looking at the Jack Frost patterns. They were. Delicate fern-leaf traces, in complicated, intricate patterns. He'd no idea frost did that. Had windows looked like that all the way through history, until

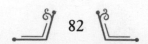

someone had got round to inventing central heating, or double glazing, or whatever it was that had stopped them?

How strange and rather wonderful. He wondered what else the history books were hiding from him.

Breakfast was toast and butter – the butter was delivered on individual pats on the sides of people's plates, so nobody took more than their fair share – and scrambled eggs and breakfast cereal. 1947 bread was something called the "National Loaf", which was small, grey and sorry-looking. It tasted like sawdust.

There were also Kellogg's Cornflakes in a white

box with no pictures on it and "Kellogg's" written in the familiar jaunty red writing, and something called Force in a box with a little man on it. There was even a jar of Marmite, with "MARMITE" written in exactly the same white letters on their red background, although the lid was made of metal, and the bottle, though still small and round, was a slightly different shape and made of glass. Alex found this almost the strangest thing of all. 1947 was a long, long time ago; it felt seriously weird to think of people eating things like cornflakes and Marmite.

The milk, however, was reassuringly old-fashioned, in proper glass bottles. Sheila immediately began clamouring for the "top of the

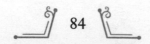

milk".

"Oh, dry up, Sheila, you little horror," Colin told her cheerfully. "You had it yesterday; it's mine and Janet's turn today."

"Although…" Janet looked anxiously at Alex and Ruby. "Perhaps Alex and Ruby *ought* to have it, as they're guests."

"We don't need milk," said Ruby hastily. They'd agreed on this strategy the night before. "We like dry cereal – we often have it at home, just as a snack. And what *is* the top of the milk, anyway?"

"Don't you have cream on top of your milk?" said Colin. "Why ever not? Don't they, on farms?"

The scrambled egg was a bit of a surprise. Alex and Ruby always had milk and cereal for breakfast

– eggs were a special treat breakfast, for holidays at Applecott House or Christmas Day. Surely people living off rations couldn't have eggs?

Alex took an enthusiastic mouthful of his and nearly spat it out, it was so disgusting. It tasted mostly like wet paste and nothing at all like egg.

Colin caught his eye and pulled a sympathetic face. "Powdered egg," he said. "I don't suppose you have to eat it living on a farm. Lucky, lucky you!"

They'd almost finished when Mrs Culpepper appeared in the doorway.

"Ten to nine, folks," she said. "Anyone for a last cup of tea before the electricity goes off?"

There was a murmur of assent from the table.

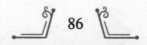 86

Alex and Ruby looked at each other. Whatever did she mean?

Granny, meanwhile, was looking at the children. "Mr Pilgrim and I usually go to church on Sundays," she said. "I don't suppose any of you lot want to come too?"

"No fear!" Colin said. "We're far too busy, Granny. Alex and Ruby are going to help us solve the highwayman's riddle. Sheila can go if she wants."

"No!" Sheila cried. "I'm going to help too! Janet *said* I could!"

"Of course you can," said Janet hurriedly. And that was that.

As they went out into the hall, Ruby grabbed Sheila and dragged her over to the corner.

"The electricity goes off?" Alex said.

"Oh yes." Sheila nodded. "Just after breakfast till twelve o'clock. Then you get two hours to make lunch in, then you have to turn it off again. We get it back at four so we can see again, but it's usually so dark by then we have to use candles for a bit anyway. That's rather jolly. It *is* rotten, though, because our cooker's electric, so you can't make a cup of tea or *anything*. You have to put the camping kettle over the fire. It's because of the coal shortages, Grandfather says."

"Wow," said Alex. "What happens if—"

But Ruby was shaking her head. "We don't have

time to worry about any of that now," she said. "We have to stop your granny going to church! Can't you pretend to be ill or something?"

"Can't *you*?" said Alex.

Ruby ignored him.

"You'd have to stop Grandfather going too," said Sheila. "And won't she just go and see her after church anyway? You can't keep both of them at home forever."

"We could lock them in the stable loft," said Ruby, then, seeing Alex's expression, she added, "I'm joking! Honestly! Look, if we can't stop Granny going, can't we send Mrs Blackstaff off somewhere? If the phones are down and she's the sort of person who organises everyone, I mean?"

"What, send her up a mountain to rescue some more snowed-in people?" said Alex doubtfully. "Why would she listen to us? How would we even know about them?"

"Well, some poor people who need soup or something. What are you looking at me like that for? That's what vicars' wives used to do in the olden days. Like in *Little Women* when they take their breakfast to the poor people. She's obviously a bossy sort if she's evacuating people off hills."

"She has to boss people," said Sheila. "She's the district visitor." They looked at her blankly. "She visits people and helps them if they need help. It's her job. Oh! I know!" Her face lit up. "We could tell her Mr Arnabus is back! That would work."

"Mr Arnabus?" said Alex. "Do I want to know?"

"He's awful," said Sheila. "He's horrible to Mrs Arnabus and all her children, and she threw him out last year and moved to Cambridge to live with her sister, and Mrs Blackstaff said good riddance to bad rubbish, and we were to tell her if he ever came back looking for them and she'd go and sort him out. She would too," she added with relish. "She caught Colin and Terence Williams taking plums from the tree in her garden and she didn't half give them what for! Mrs Arnabus's old house is all the way out on Forest Park Road; it'd take her an age to get there and back. I'll go now!" She jumped up and ran for her boots.

Alex said, "You'll just go? On your own?"

Sheila looked surprised. "It's not far."

"I know..." Applecott House was right next to the church, and the vicarage was in the next lane. "But..."

Alex and Ruby hadn't been allowed out alone without their mum and dad until they were much older than Sheila. Alex had been nine before he'd been allowed past the end of their road on his own. And even now he had to tell someone where he was going, and when he'd be back, and take his phone so his mum or dad could call him if he was late. Sheila looked about six. Surely she wasn't allowed to just *go*?

But apparently she was.

Colin put his head round the living-room door

and said, "Hullo! Where's Sheila gone?"

And when Alex said she'd gone to the vicarage, he just shrugged and said, "Oh. Well, she'd better buck up if she wants to help."

Mrs Blackstaff apparently didn't think it was odd either. When Sheila came running back, her hair full of new snow, she beamed at them triumphantly. "Mission accomplished!" she said.

Colin raised his eyebrows. "Do I want to know?" he said. "No, on second thoughts, don't answer that. Can we get started *now*?"

There was a new wood fire burning in the living room. The children sat down by the hearth, pulled out the bit of paper and stared at it gloomily.

I've fallen for you,

Little apple-dweller.

They cannot force us apart.

I'll keep your secret hidden.

"It sounds like a love poem," said Alex. "*Apple-dweller* – maybe that's Applecott House? But it can't be, I suppose."

"Maybe it is," said Ruby. "*I'll keep your secret hidden.* Maybe it just means he wasn't going to tell her where the treasure was. Maybe it was all just a joke on her dad all along."

"Except *Mum solved it*," said Colin.

"We don't think the *I* is the highwayman at all," said Janet. "We think it's the thing the treasure was hidden in. Like – *I've fallen for you* – we thought that might be a fallen tree maybe. It could even be an apple tree. And you can't force the treasure and the tree apart, so it's going to stay hidden. That would fit."

"Except a fallen tree wouldn't still be here a hundred years later," said Ruby. "A live tree maybe, but not a dead one. Would it?" she added uncertainly. Trees weren't Ruby's strong point.

Alex shrugged. "Maybe it fell and kept growing," he said. "Maybe it's one of the trees in the orchard at Applecott House!"

"Except it isn't," said Colin. "We looked. We looked at them all, and they're just trees. Most of them aren't even old!"

"Are there any big old fallen trees anywhere round here?" said Ruby.

The children shook their heads.

"No!" said Sheila. "We asked *everyone*. Nobody knew of *any*."

"Oh well," said Ruby. "I thought you said it was something that only worked in winter anyway?"

"We don't know that," said Janet. "That was just Colin's idea. But it was a jolly good idea, I thought. Like an island maybe. You couldn't get there unless the water froze."

"Couldn't you use a boat?"

"Well, there might be rocks or something. Or rapids! Boats can't get everywhere. Dad's in the navy, you know, and there are plenty of places destroyers can't go. I don't see why little boats would be any different."

Alex supposed that made sense. He said, interested, "I suppose it wouldn't be too far from Applecott House then, would it? I mean, they didn't have cars and things in highwayman times, did they?"

"They had horses," Ruby pointed out. "You could get miles and miles and miles on a horse."

"Not *so* many miles in winter," said Alex doubtfully. Horses weren't *his* strong point. "Well, anyway," said Ruby, "we could look it up on a map – see if there are any inaccessible islands nearby—" She stopped. "What?" she said.

Colin and Janet were frowning at her.

"Thing is," said Janet, "we *have* looked – I mean, at maps and things. And there simply *isn't*

anything. And Grandfather and Granny couldn't think of anything it might be either. But I thought, well, rivers have little rocks and so forth in them, don't they? And they wouldn't show on a map. So if it's somewhere the highwayman and his girlfriend went to together, she'd know at once which one he was talking about, but how can we?"

"Because *Mum found it*," said Colin.

Alex frowned at the piece of paper. "There must be more of a clue in here then," he said. "It *can't* be just somewhere they'd know, he'd have to actually be trying to tell her where it is properly in code. Like that line about an apple-dweller – if you were writing a code, that wouldn't just mean *my girlfriend who lives at Applecott House*, it would

mean *something*. And so would everything else.
We've just got to figure out *what*."

"Oh?" said Ruby. "Is that all? That'll be easy
then."

And they stared at the riddle in gloom.

CHAPTER SIX
FALLING

"This is useless!" Colin said at last, pushing the piece of paper away. They'd been talking nothing but riddles for the past hour. "If I spend another minute looking at it, I'll go potty. Let's do something else. Let's have a snowball fight. We

might have a pretty decent one with five of us."

A snowball fight! Alex felt a little leap of excitement. In all his nearly eleven years it had snowed enough for a snowball fight precisely twice. The first time he'd been a toddler, too small to remember. The last time, he'd been seven. Far too long ago. Climate change, he was beginning to

feel, had a lot to answer for.

That morning's snowball fight on the lawn at Applecott House was something he thought he'd remember forever. There weren't teams, or rules, or anything except a mad, glorious, sweaty rough and tumble in the snow. It was wonderful.

"That," he said, as they tumbled into the kitchen for lunch, "was amazing."

"It was only a snowball fight," said Janet, looking surprised.

They ate lunch in the kitchen with Mrs Culpepper, because Granny and Grandfather were eating at church then going to a beetle drive, whatever that was. Alex really, really hoped they were racing beetles; he hoped this so much that he didn't want to ask what it really was, as he knew he'd be disappointed.

Lunch was bread and dripping, which was grey and slimy.

"*Dripping?*" said Ruby sceptically.

"It's all the bits of juice off the joint," said Sheila.

"Ugh!" said Ruby. "That's disgusting!"

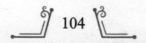

Alex wished she wouldn't. He was beginning to hate how scornful she was of everything 1947.

"It tastes quite nice actually," he said, trying his slice. "It's no worse than pork scratchings."

"I think you should jolly well stop being so feeble," said Colin, with a glance at Ruby. "Granny and Grandfather have been awful bricks about you coming here. They're sharing all our rations, and you're just being a beast about it. The least you could do is be grateful!"

"I'll say!" said Sheila, sitting up in her chair.

"It's not that I'm not grateful—" Ruby began. Alex kicked her, and she stopped. "All right," she said. "I'm sorry. I just – how you *cope*? Without sweets or cakes or – or anything?"

"It's completely putrid," Sheila agreed. "When I'm grown up, I'm going to live in – in America and eat whatever I want."

Ruby picked up her bread and took a small, rather mutinous bite.

"It's not … *bad*, I suppose," she said doubtfully. But she didn't sound convinced.

After lunch, they dragged themselves back to the riddle again. Sheila gave a big dramatic sigh – "This is *so boring!*" – and pulled out a box of Meccano to play with instead. Alex had never seen Meccano before, and would have rather liked a go himself, but Colin slapped the riddle determinedly down on the table, and he turned his attention towards it.

"So something that falls," he said for the thousandth time. "Or something fallen. Something that can't be forced apart. That you can only get to in winter. It *must* be an island."

"Yeah, yeah, we know," said Ruby. "With rapids. Cos there are *so* many rapids in Suffolk."

"It doesn't have to be rapids," said Janet, looking hurt. "Maybe – maybe there's a waterfall. That you can't take a boat down. Or – or get behind maybe! Maybe there's a cave behind a waterfall. I say! Waterfalls fall! Fallen – it's a waterfall!"

"Crikey, that fits!" said Colin. "Golly! Oh, what about 'force us apart', though? That's not a waterfall."

"Yes, it is!" said Ruby. "Force is a Viking word for waterfall – there are loads of waterfalls called 'force' where we live. I mean –" she caught Janet's eye – "where we used to live. Up north. Where there were lots of Vikings," she finished rather lamely, but fortunately Colin wasn't listening.

"What waterfall, though? There are loads around here – we can't check them all. Well, I suppose we *could*, but it would take an age, and it's not as though we could even bicycle in this weather. And what about *little apple-dweller*, what's that got to do with anything?"

"It's a clue to what waterfall it is," said Alex at once. "It must be. What else lives in apples besides Pilgrims?"

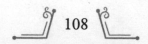

"Worms!" said Sheila. "And maggots!"

"Sheila, you are a story," said Colin. "As if anyone would call a waterfall Maggot Fall."

"They might!" said Sheila. "If – if—" But the others weren't listening.

"Rotten bits," said Ruby. "And vitamins. Though the highwayman wouldn't know about those, I suppose."

"We need a map," said Colin. He bolted out of the room and was back almost immediately with a very old-fashioned-looking Ordnance Survey map with a cardboard cover. He spread it open on the table and the children crowded round it. Inside it looked – unsurprisingly, Alex supposed – very like the maps his parents used on country walks.

"Look at the rivers," said Ruby, but Colin was already reading the names out.

"Glass Falls. Sedley Falls. Blue Foss. This is hopeless! None of these are even slightly maggoty."

"Let's look further away," said Janet. "He never said he hid it *near* here." But none of the other waterfalls were any better. They folded out the map and peered at all the lakes and rivers and ponds they could find. Nothing.

"I reckon it's something obscure, like it's Blue Foss because there was a dog called Blue who dwelt at Applecott House," said Ruby at last, in disgust.

"But *Mum—*" Janet insisted.

"Oh, who knows what it means?" said Ruby.

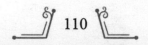

She pushed her chair away in frustration. "Do you want to play some more cards or something? Even snap is better than this."

There was a big cupboard in the corner of the room with the cards and other games in it. Ruby wandered over and began looking through the things piled up there. Colin followed, and Sheila jumped up and started clamouring to play Monopoly. There seemed to be a tacit agreement that the riddle was to be left, at least for now.

Alex glanced at Janet. She looked down at the table, fighting back tears. Somehow – although this whole quest had been Colin's idea – it seemed to matter to her much more.

"Please don't worry," he said. "*I* don't think

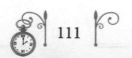

apple-dweller means the girlfriend. It's like in crosswords." Alex's mum loved cryptic crosswords, and although Alex privately thought they sounded impossible, he loved the *idea* of them. "You don't put something in a crossword unless you need it to solve the clue. It must mean something."

"But there isn't anything it *could* mean!" said Janet.

Alex frowned at the map. "One thing Mum says about crosswords," he said, "is that if you can't solve the clue the right way round, you need to look at what the answer might be and try to work out why. Like, if you look at the letters you've got in the clue, you think of words that might fit there,

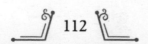

and then you try to figure out why they might be the answer."

Janet looked puzzled, so he said, "Like, the answer might be Glass Falls. So why might glass be an apple-dweller? It can't be, so that isn't right. Or Sedley – hey, Sedley! Seed! You get seeds in apples, don't you? That's it!"

"Oh!" Janet's face blazed. "Oh, it must be! You're right. Look!" She rushed over to the bookcases and pulled out an enormous old book. "Look, it's here somewhere, I know it is! Oh, there! Look!"

It was a very old-looking map of the village. The waterfall was marked in funny, twisty old-fashioned writing. *Seedley Falls.*

"Seedley! Look! The old name for the fall!"

"Oh!" said Colin, who had come up behind them to see what the fuss was about.

"And Sedley Falls are right here in the village – it couldn't be easier!" Janet said excitedly. "They're frightfully fierce too; you couldn't just lower yourself down on a rope – you'd be battered to death."

"That's true!" said Alex.

He knew Sedley Falls – they were a "local attraction". Aunt Joanna had a leaflet about them on her hall table for the bed and breakfast guests. The Victorian Pilgrims had gone ice skating there. The current in the river above the falls was very fierce; there were strict notices on the bank above about how swimming was forbidden. He tried to imagine climbing down the falls. With a rope, you wouldn't fall, but the force of the water would pound you against the rock of the cliffs behind. He shivered.

"I say!" said Colin. His face was ablaze. "And all Mum and Dad's rock-climbing stuff is still in the stable loft. We could go there now! It couldn't be easier!"

"Rock climbing?" Alex was alarmed. He didn't know the first thing about rock climbing, but he was pretty sure it wasn't something children were supposed to do in the snow.

"Oh, it's fine." Colin waved his hand. "Me and Janet have done heaps of rock climbing with Dad. Well, some. A bit anyway. Let's go now!"

"You *what*?" said Ruby.

"You don't have to come if you're scared," Colin said hastily. "You can stay here and look after Sheila and cover for us with Granny and Grandfather."

"Excuse *me*," said Ruby. "I'm not scared! I'm being sensible! You are *insane*! It's the middle of the coldest winter in three hundred years! The cliffs are going to be covered in ice! You aren't mountaineers! You're kids! And even mountaineers wouldn't go out in weather like this! They've got too much sense!"

"That's not true," said Colin. He was wearing a rather mutinous expression, which Alex recognised with a sinking heart. Ruby had a very similar face, usually worn when about to do something she knew was a bad idea. "Loads of big mountains always have snow on top, and plenty of mountaineers climb those!"

"But they're mountaineers!" Ruby cried. "They aren't kids!" She swung round to Alex. "Alex! Tell them what a stupid idea this is!"

"I dunno..." Alex knew she was right; of course she was. But... "Don't you think this is what the mi— I mean, don't you think maybe we're *supposed* to help them. Because, well, because," he finished vaguely.

"Maybe what we have to do is stop them killing themselves!" said Ruby.

But Alex didn't think so. "If we hadn't been

here, they wouldn't even have solved that riddle," he pointed out.

Ruby sighed. "*Fine!*" she said. "But no way are you leaving me behind."

"Or me!" said Sheila hopefully.

Colin gave a "ha!".

Ruby glared at Janet, who said, "Oh, for heaven's sake! What does it matter who comes, so long as we *go*?"

CHAPTER SEVEN
THE SEARCHING

They fetched the climbing gear from the stable loft, dressed themselves in every bit of warm clothing they possessed, and set off.

At first, the walking was easy enough. The path from the house had been cleared that morning, and although the road was still covered in snow there was a small track along the side of the road, dug out for pedestrians.

Under his jacket and woolly hat, Alex wore several jumpers: one belonging to Colin, the other to Grandfather. He also wore a rather prickly hand-knitted scarf belonging to Granny and a pair of gloves that Colin had outgrown and which had a hole in the finger. But it was odd; he wasn't nearly as cold as he'd expected to be. He was pretty warm actually; his jacket was unzipped and he'd stuffed his hat in his pocket. Keeping moving seemed to make all the difference; hanging around outside waiting for Colin and Janet to find the climbing gear, he'd been freezing.

Colin had an old-fashioned haversack with all the ropes and so forth in it. Ruby had another with a Thermos of hot tea, some apples, a couple of decidedly home-made-looking biscuits and the tail end of Colin and Janet's sweet ration. Sheila – much to her disgust – had been left at home. Alex was glad of that, at least. She looked far too little to be climbing up icy cliffs.

Alex knew he ought to be scared, and he was, a bit, in a vague sort of way. But it didn't feel scary, not yet. Mostly what it was, was beautiful. The bare, silent village, the black silhouettes of the trees on the skyline, the rooks in the rookery. The wintery snow-covered world, both strange and familiar. And it was *so much* like something out of an Arthur Ransome novel, he kept wanting to do little jumps of excitement. Buried treasure! In the snow! Haversacks and sou'westers and gumboots!

"I say," he muttered to himself, and resisted the urge to giggle.

He and Ruby knew Sedley Falls, though not well. It was one waterfall really, at the edge of a lake. There were ducks, and trees, and wooden noticeboards telling you about local wildlife and picnic tables. In summer you got families, and at other times of the year you got dog walkers and joggers, and toddlers feeding the ducks. It was a totally ordinary, boring, well-used bit of land, not at all the sort of place you'd expect to find buried treasure.

In the middle of winter, though... In the middle of winter it was something else entirely. It was bare and white and empty, and almost otherworldly. The lake was frozen, making it feel like something from a film or a book, something not quite real. It had been frozen in Victorian village too. It had been magical then as well.

The path from the village meandered through the trees and then along the shore of the lake. At the far end the shoreline tapered to a point, where the water poured over the edge of the cliffs and down into the river below. These were the falls. They were looking down on them, of course, which made them harder to see, but as far as

Alex could tell, Colin and Janet were right: it was completely iced up, the water caught mid-fall. It was weirdly beautiful and eerily silent.

It was also – which Alex had forgotten about – completely inaccessible. The lake was edged with the top of the cliffs, and the edge was not only precarious but completely frozen. At the bottom of the waterfall the water quickly spread outwards to form the wide frozen river. To get to the top of the waterfall they'd either have to walk on the frozen water of the lake or clamber on the very edge of the frozen clifftop. To get to the bottom of the falls they'd have to walk on the icy river.

"How are we going to get there?" he said.

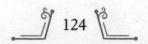

Colin and Janet looked at him like he was mad.

"We'll walk, of course," said Colin.

"On the ice!" Alex was taken aback. Ice in modern Dalton was absolutely not for walking on. Their parents had impressed on them never to step even on a frozen duck pond, as it would not hold their weight. The only time Alex had seen a frozen lake, except in cartoons, was in Victorian Dalton. But people had skated on that.

Would this 1947 lake be safe? He supposed it must be, if it really was the coldest winter in three hundred years. But how slippery was it? If they fell over, would they go straight over the cliff?

"It's perfectly safe," said Colin. "People have been skating on it for weeks – honestly they have.

You couldn't skate now with all this snow, but they brush that off, and then it's super. We come most years."

"If we're going to go, hadn't we better go?" said Ruby. She looked anxiously at the sky. "I mean, it's going to get dark soon too…"

"Right-oh," said Colin. "C'mon."

He picked up his knapsack, heaved it on to his shoulders and headed straight towards where the edge of the lake must be – it was hard to tell under the snow. Gingerly he put first one foot on the ice, then another. It showed no signs of cracking.

"Are you *sure*?" said Ruby.

Colin jumped up and down. Not even a creak.

"If you don't want to come…" he said.

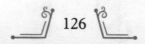

"We're coming," said Ruby. "But don't blame *me* if we drown."

They picked their way across the lake towards the top of the falls carefully, making sure not to slip. *Crunch* went the snow beneath their feet. *Crunch. Crunch. Crunch.*

Inside Alex's coat it was warm, but his face was raw and the air was icy.

The clouds above were heavy and grey. It was still light, but Ruby was right; it wouldn't be for much longer. They'd probably be coming home in the dark. Alex shivered. They really could kill themselves, he realised suddenly. Colin actually was going to try to climb over the frozen cliff.

And then they were there at the top of the waterfall, and suddenly it was all very real.

Neither Alex nor Ruby had done much rock climbing before. Alex had had a go on a climbing wall on the Year Six Residential and hadn't got very far up. They'd also done abseiling, which had been a lot more fun, though he wasn't sure he remembered enough of how to do it to want to try here in the middle of nowhere with no friendly instructor in case it all went wrong.

And, anyway, was abseiling a thing people did in 1947? They obviously did rock climbing, because the children's parents had been rock climbers. But what sort of equipment did they have? Was it really safe?

Colin was taking off his knapsack. He pulled out an old bit of carpet and a length of long rope.

"Is ... is that *it*?" said Ruby, horrified.

"Well, Dad's got harnesses and things," said Colin, "but they're all a bit big for us, really."

"Oh," said Alex. He looked at the carpet. "Er, what's that for?"

"You put it over the edge," said Colin,

demonstrating. "It stops the rope fraying on the rock and breaking."

Ruby squealed. "*Breaking*?"

"It won't, though – don't worry." Colin grinned. "Don't fuss. We've done loads of this sort of stuff with Dad."

Alex looked at Janet. He'd expected her to be as nervous as he was. Instead she looked completely calm. Did 1947 girls do loads of dangling off cliffs on ropes? He knew the girls in *Swallows and Amazons* did, but he'd never thought that was *normal*.

"You are all mad," Ruby said. "Mad! And I'm even madder for coming along with you."

Alex had to admit that Colin did seem to know

what he was doing. He tied the rope to a tree with some pretty professional-looking knots, and then looped it round another tree and did the same again.

"Just to be sure," he said, winking at Ruby.

Then he took the length of carpet and spread it out over the cliff edge. Then he peered down thoughtfully for a few moments. Alex shivered. There wasn't much light left. Should they come back tomorrow? But, no, if they did that, it would be too late. Granny would have had time to go and find Mrs Blackstaff, to go to Ipswich and realise that Alex and Ruby Jones had never existed. It had to be now.

"I think …" Colin said, "since you two have

never done this before, we won't all go down. We'll send Janet down on the rope, and she can tell us if there's anything there or not. Much safer."

Alex supposed it was. He wasn't sure if he felt relieved or disappointed. Probably relieved, he decided. Ruby, for all her protestations, definitely looked a bit put out.

Colin took the end of the rope and tied it round Janet's waist and under her legs. It looked pretty sturdy. He spooled out a length of rope for her to hold, then wrapped the next length round his body and arm.

"See?" he said. "It's called a body belay. I'm going to sit here – braced, like this. And then Janet goes down, and I let out more rope as she goes, and then if she falls, I take the weight."

"And can you?" said Ruby doubtfully. "I mean, she's person-sized."

"Oh yes," said Colin. "Do try to climb if you can, Jan, but if you have to let me lower you down, let me know."

"Right," said Janet. She didn't sound at all anxious.

Alex allowed himself to be a bit reassured.

"Careful now," Colin said.

Janet nodded. Then she took off her gloves, stuffed them into her pocket, and began to lower herself over the cliff edge.

They waited. Alex was beginning to get cold. His

face was the coldest – the air really did feel like ice – but the chill was beginning to bite into the rest of him too. He gave Ruby a meaningful look, which said *This is mad, isn't it?*

Ruby shrugged. She stuck her gloved hands under her armpits and jumped up and down.

"If I get chilblains, I am going to be *so annoyed*," she said.

It was hard to see what was going on below them, but Janet didn't seem to be in any difficulties.

"It's not too bad," she called up. "It's just jolly icy – I'm glad we've got the rope. Oh, this bit's harder. Hang on, I think – no, no, it's all right. I've done it. Golly! The waterfall's bigger than it looks when you're right up against it." There was

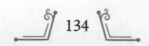

a long pause.

"Everything all right?" Ruby called down.

There was a scrabbling noise, then: "*Yes!* Yes, it's here – a real cave! We were right!"

"But what about the treasure? And the necklace? Is it there?"

"I don't know! Hang on—"

Colin played out more rope. They waited. And then, at last, there was Janet's voice again.

"I can't tell! It's not very deep, but there are rocks and things at the back – I think some of the wall must have come down. There's a hole and I *think* I can see something at the back, sort of glittering behind the rocks, but I can't get my hand in."

Colin made a noise of frustration.

Ruby said, "But we *can't* have come all this way for it not to work. We *can't*."

"I was wondering," Janet's voice called up. "D'you think Alex could come down? His hands are smaller than mine – he might…"

They all looked at Alex.

He swallowed. "All right," he said. "I mean, OK. Sure."

"You don't have to," said Ruby. She looked uncharacteristically nervous. Was *Ruby* worried about him? Really?

"Actually," he said, "I think I probably do."

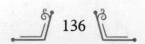

CHAPTER EIGHT
THE FINDING

There was only one rope, so they had to wait
while Janet untied her makeshift harness and
Colin pulled the rope up to the top of the cliff. He
fastened it on to Alex's stomach and tugged on
the knot – it seemed to hold.

"Ready?" he said, and Alex nodded. Ready.

The first part of the descent, as Janet had said, wasn't too hard – no harder than the scrambling they did on the cliffs at the seaside. The ice made everything about a hundred times more scary, though; Alex was grateful he was wearing an old pair of Colin's boots instead of his trainers. And he wasn't *entirely* sure he trusted Colin to catch him if he fell. It all felt very amateurish compared to the fancy equipment they'd had on the Year Six Residential.

And about halfway down, the climbing got harder. Alex could see where he was *supposed* to put his feet – Janet's footprints were imprinted in the snow – but Janet was taller than he was,

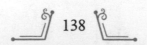

and the rock looked worrying slippery and the footholds alarmingly far away. And his hands were numb and stiff with cold.

"All right?" Janet shouted.

"Just give me a minute," he said. He couldn't go back up, not now, not so close, but...

"You *have* got me if I fall, haven't you?" he called up.

"Definitely!" Colin yelled back.

"It's not as hard as it looks." Janet's head appeared below him – really not that far down. "Put your foot out and lean forward – not too fast – and you'll land there. And then it's easy."

Easy, thought Alex. *All right for her to say.* But he took a deep breath, and did as she said – and then, suddenly, there he was, on the next foothold, and there was Janet standing in, yes, in a shallow cave behind the waterfall, and all he had to do was clamber down over the boulders to join her.

"All right?" she said.

He nodded a little breathlessly and took a step towards her, his boots slipping on the floor of the cave.

"It's icy!" he said.

It was. In here, where the snow could not reach, the ground was covered in a thin sheet of ice.

"I know," she said. "I wish we'd brought more rope."

He had to agree. One slip and she could easily fall to her death.

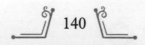

She shone her torch back into the cave. "Isn't it terrific, though? A secret hideaway!"

Secretly, Alex thought it was rather an anticlimax. They were standing in a small, rather shallow cave, just tall enough to stand up in. It tailed off behind them into the darkness, but when Janet tipped her torch up it became clear that it didn't go back very far at all – perhaps three or four metres. The walls shrank quickly, making the space rather claustrophobic.

"It's just here," said Janet, stepping forward carefully, her hands clutching the side of the cave. "Look!"

The back of the cave sharpened into a point. Here, it was harder to see and harder to search.

Not only was it darker, but there were boulders
and spurs of rock in a muddled heap on the floor.

"There's been a landslide or something," said
Alex. "There's no way we'll be able to clear all
this."

"I know," said Janet. "But I'm sure it's the right place. Look!" She crouched down beside the heap of rocks and shone her torch into the hole. "Can you see – there – something glimmering?"

Alex looked. He wasn't sure – it wasn't at all clear in the darkness, and yet, perhaps, at the back was something that looked like it might be gold, shining…

"We'll never reach that," he said. "Not without proper stone-moving equipment – and we'd never get that down the cliff."

"No, I know," said Janet, "but look here—" She moved the torch and shone it into another crack in the stones further down. "There's something there! Isn't there?"

Alex bent down and peered into the darkness. There *was* something. Something silvery glittering on the floor of the cave, half beneath the pile of rocks.

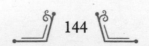

"It's caught, I think – under the pile."

"I know, but if you could pull… I tried but my hand's too big. I thought yours might be smaller—"

Alex slid his hand between the hole. It was a tight squeeze, but it *did* go.

"I don't— No, hang on…"

His fingers touched something cold and wet. He tugged but it wouldn't come. "The chain's caught under some rocks or something."

"Can't you break it? If we could just *show* it to her – so she knew Mum really *did* lose it—"

Alex tugged. At first he thought nothing was going to happen, then there was a *snap* as the chain broke and he fell backwards. "Oof!"

It was a tarnished silver locket on a long silver chain. It looked, Alex thought, like rather a dull thing to have caused so much trouble, more like something you saw sold for a couple of pounds in antique shops than buried treasure.

"It's the lost necklace," he said. "It must be."

"Halloo! Halloo! What's happening down there?"

Ruby was calling from the top of the cliff. They went out to the edge of the cave.

"We found it!" Alex called.

Ruby and Colin's faces appeared over the edge of the cliff above them.

"Then come back up!" Ruby yelled. "It's freezing! And it's going to be dark soon!"

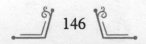

Alex waved to show he understood, then he and Janet looked at each other.

"Do you want to go first, or shall I?" she said.

Alex hesitated. He would have liked Janet to go first, so she could tell him where to put his feet and reassure him that the ascent was possible. But on the other hand… He looked doubtfully at the knots on his harness. Could he retie them himself down here all alone, if Janet took the rope up first? Would they be safe?

"I think I'd better," he said.

The cave was protected by a shallow overhang, now mostly covered in ice. Alex gave the rope a cautious tug, wanting to be sure that Colin was ready to take his weight.

The rope held. He moved towards the edge of the ledge. The rope pulled against the overhang. And …

With a sickening noise that sounded worryingly like *crack* …

Two of the three strands of the rope snapped, leaving Alex supported by one last, rather perilous, strand.

He said, "Oh!" and sat down in a hurry.

And the last remaining strand of rope snapped.

Leaving Alex and Janet alone halfway down the icy cliff.

There was a short, rather furious, argument.

Colin said it was Alex's fault for being so stupid.

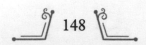

Ruby said it was Colin's fault for not bringing a spare rope, and how exactly was Alex supposed to have stopped it happening anyway?

Colin said they should climb up without the rope and it would probably be fine.

Alex said no. No way. There was ice. And snow. It would be a ridiculous thing to do, and they'd deserve to get killed. And it would be Colin's fault if they did. Every time Colin tried to tell him it would all be fine, he remembered that tricky bit where Janet had had to talk him through it. He remembered how icy the handholds had been. And how far it was down to the bottom.

"No," he said. "No. No. No way."

Janet said, blimey! It wasn't hard. Somebody

would have to go and get another rope and come and rescue them. And could they do it quickly, because they were standing in an ice cave, it was getting really cold, and it was only going to get worse?

So, in the end, that's what they did. Ruby and Colin sent down their coats and their hats on what was left of the rope – Ruby insisted on this – and they crunched off back towards the house. Alex and Janet stood on the ledge, by the frozen waterfall, hugging themselves to keep warm, trying not to wonder how long the rescue would be, and if it would come before darkness fell.

It was very, very cold. And it was only going to get colder.

At the other end of the village, in the hallway at Applecott House, the house was dark and very still. Granny and Grandfather were still at the beetle drive. Mrs Culpepper was in the kitchen, trying to work out how to stretch the remains of the week's rations to feed eight. The fire in the living room had sputtered and finally died, and Sheila wasn't allowed to touch it. She sat alone on the bottom step, wrapped in a blanket with only a doll and a candle in a jam jar to keep her company, and cried.

The others had been gone for *hours*. Hours and hours. Sheila wasn't very good at estimating time, and right now it felt as though they'd been gone for her whole *life*. Surely something dreadful must have happened to them, and they'd never be coming back? It didn't occur to Sheila that in this case it was her job to sound the alarm. She was a little girl. It was the grown-ups' job to sort out problems. Children just did as they were told, and Colin had told her not to tell the grown-ups where they were. So she didn't. She just sat there and wept.

How she *hated* being the youngest, always left out of things! How she hated this miserable midwinter world, where you weren't even allowed to turn on the electricity. How she hated having no mother, and a father on the other side of the world. Wouldn't he *ever* come home?

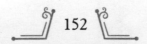

Sheila's memories of her father were somewhat confused. She had a photograph of him in navy uniform that sat on her windowsill, but he looked very faraway and handsome, like someone in a war film, not like a real person at all. He sent them presents from Japan – little toys and sweets and Japanese dolls in kimonos. To Sheila he was more than half a fairy-tale creature.

"Perhaps Janet and Colin will be killed," she wept. She didn't really understand how treasure could be hidden behind the waterfall – in her mind it was locked in a sort of strongbox, like an air-raid shelter or the pillboxes on the Suffolk coast. But the danger of the frozen waterfall was very clear to her. She could picture it in her mind:

the water perfect and frozen, Janet and Colin and Alex and Ruby stepping into the space behind and then – in Sheila's mind this happened all at once – the ice dissolving in a sudden rush, and the children trapped forever behind falling water.

Sheila had lost her mother, and to all intents and purposes her father, but she had always had Janet, fussing over her dirty face and her scuffed shoes, and she had always had Colin, calling her an "ass" and a "goose", and then stepping in and doing something marvellous, like making her a Christmas tree out of crêpe paper the year she'd cried because children in books always had trees at Christmas and in wartime they couldn't.

There was a knock at the door. Sheila, still

weeping, made no move to open it. Mrs Culpepper could get it, she thought, but Mrs Culpepper had just that moment gone out to the stable yard to fetch water from the pump and could not hear.

There was a pause and then a click, and the door opened. Sheila looked up, shocked.

A man was standing there. He was wearing a greatcoat and what Janet or Colin would have recognised as a demob suit, but Sheila just thought was an unusually new set of clothes. Over his shoulder was a holdall. He looked, Sheila thought, a little bit like Colin and a little bit like her grandfather. His face was tanned and his eyes, behind their spectacles, were worried. Sheila, staring at him, felt as though she knew him somehow, though her mind – fugged with tears – couldn't quite place how.

"Who are you?" she whispered.

And the man, as some part of her had known he would, replied, "You're Sheila, aren't you? I'm your father. I've come home."

CHAPTER NINE
HOMECOMING

"I did try to call," he said, "but all the phone lines are down in the snow." And then: "Sheila ... what's wrong? What's happened?"

So she told him.

Ruby and Colin were coming home. But without coats and hats – even going as fast as they could manage in the snow – the wind cut right through them. Their faces were stiff and raw and icy to the touch.

It was hard to hurry when the path was thick with snow. Their footprints were still there from the outward journey, which did help. But it was such an unnatural movement, walking through thick snow – lift your foot up out of the snow print, plant it into the next print, careful not to topple yourself, hoick your other foot out and start the same thing over again.

If only, Ruby thought desperately, they could just run and run and run and run. A cave of ice. It had a horribly final sound to it. She tried to think of Eskimos and igloos and Arctic explorers. But Eskimos had fire and fur, and Arctic explorers had layers of expensive clothes, and all Alex and Janet had were ancient overcoats and woolly hats. *The mirror wouldn't have brought us here if we weren't going to be safe*, she thought, but it sounded hollow even to herself. Ruby loved the mirror, but she had never felt safe inside it. She didn't feel at all safe now. It was cold. Her brother's time was running out. And it was growing dark.

And then the skies above them opened, and the snow began to fall.

Even in two sets of coats and hats, the ledge

behind the waterfall was very cold. Alex knew you had to keep moving to keep warm, but it was difficult; the rock was slippery with ice, so you could hardly jump up and down or run on the spot. The possibility of slipping and falling to their deaths was far too likely – and horrifying – to think about. He windmilled his arms around a few times, but he felt vaguely ridiculous. All his instincts were to huddle closer, tensing himself against the cold.

Janet didn't even try. She wrapped her arms round her stomach and crouched on the rock, head bent forward.

"Are you all right?" Alex said.

She nodded. "You don't think... It's not cold

enough to *die*, is it? People die of exposure, don't they?"

"I'm sure it isn't," said Alex, but he wasn't sure at all. Even with all the layers of coats and scarves and gloves, it was unbearably cold.

"I just…" Janet rocked backwards and forwards. "I can't stop thinking about Sheila. I promised Mum I'd look after her, and … well, I know I'm not very good at it, but I *do* try. If something happens to me … I don't know what she'd do. She's only little."

"Nothing's going to happen to you," said Alex, more confidently than he felt. He wondered if he should tell Janet about the magic mirror, but it sounded so implausible here. He couldn't imagine that she would possibly believe him. "And she's got your granny and your granddad, hasn't she? They're her mum and dad really, aren't they? And your dad, when he gets home."

"It's my job too, though," said Janet. "You're the youngest, so you wouldn't understand. Big sisters have to help. It's like … like making your bed in the morning, or giving the servants Christmas presents."

Alex had never made his bed in his life – mornings in his house were always a mad scramble to get out of the door and off to breakfast club and work. And Ruby had never looked after him either – although she was only two years older than he was, so he supposed it was different. But

Janet looked so worried he didn't argue.

"Do you remember your dad?" he said instead. "I mean, properly?"

"Oh yes!" Janet lifted her head. Her eyes in her pale little face were alight. "I was five when he joined up. I remember heaps about him. And he was in a camp at Ipswich until I was seven – he used to come over and see us on his free afternoons and take us out for picnics and to the beach and so forth. And he writes to us all the time, lovely long letters all about Japan, and the funny things that happen to him, and... Oh!" Her voice caught, as though she were going to cry. "Oh, he's just—" She stopped in confusion. Then, in a low voice, she said, "Well, I just wish he'd come home, that's all."

Alex – like everybody else – had done evacuees at school. Getting on a train with a label round your neck. Going to live in the countryside. He'd even written a pretend postcard home from an evacuee, all about how amazing cows and sheep and green fields were. But what he hadn't ever realised before was how *long* the war had been. Six years – that was *ages*. It was most of his life. And then an extra year and a bit (the war had started in September, he knew) waiting for your dad to come home. Just the thought of being apart from Mum for a couple of months was hard enough. To be apart for years and years… Well. It was… Well, it was dizzying.

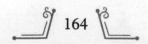

What must it be like to be Janet's father, missing most of your children's childhoods? What must it be like to be Janet?

"You must miss him," he said awkwardly, and Janet nodded.

"Oh yes," she said simply. And then she was quiet.

And outside the cave the snow began to fall.

The children's father was halfway down the lane to the waterfall when the snow came. He wore his greatcoat and his black boots, and he had a knapsack over one shoulder with hot-water bottles, and rope, and blankets, and hot tea, and bandages, just in case. He had sent the astonished

Mrs Culpepper into the village to find the children's grandparents and raise the alarm. And now here he was, walking once more through the familiar lanes of his childhood.

He looked up and saw the snow tumbling through the air like a hundred thousand feathers from a thousand feather bedspreads, all shaken out at once by a thousand celestial housewives. Despite himself, he felt a rush of joy at it all, the giddy childhood joy of snowy mornings and frozen rivers and icicles on the eaves of the houses. Sleigh bells and sledges and skates on the lake! Snow! Snow!

Then he remembered his mission, and his children on the cliff, and he put down his head and quickened his pace.

Colin and Ruby saw him coming before he saw them. A man, head bent against the snow. Ruby tugged on Colin's sleeve.

"We should ask him for help," she said. "Maybe he lives round here and he's got some rope ... or perhaps he's got a car... Do you know him?"

"Hmm." Colin screwed up his eyes and tried to focus on the bent figure. *Did* he know him? He didn't look like anyone from the village. And yet ... there was something familiar about his walk. Something about the way he held his head. "I'm not... Perhaps..."

Ruby stared at him. "Well?" she said. "Do you

know him, or don't you? Colin? *Colin!*"

"I've got some tea and biscuits in my bag," said Janet. She took the knapsack off – moving slowly and awkwardly, as though it hurt her. Alex thought he understood. Even just moving your arm away from your body meant losing heat. His arms and legs were stiff, and he couldn't feel his fingers any more. Or his toes.

"There," said Janet. The biscuits were home-made and rather healthy-looking, wrapped up in what looked like greaseproof paper, but Alex ate them anyway. They did help a bit. And the tea was wonderful.

"They can't be too long now, can they?" she

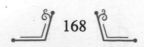

said.

Alex wasn't sure. He didn't think they'd actually been gone very long at all, though it felt like ages.

"I dunno…" he said doubtfully, but Janet grabbed his arm.

"Listen!"

"What?"

"Can't you hear it? There's someone there – I'm certain there is. Oh, do listen!"

Alex tried. *Was* there someone? He couldn't be sure, but Janet's little face was full of hope.

"Hello!" she called. "Hello! Is anyone there? Help! Oh, please help us!"

"Help!" Alex shouted.

There was a scuffle on the clifftop, and a chunk

of snow fell down across the cave mouth. They scrambled to their feet, then froze as they heard Colin's cheery call from above.

"Ahoy down there!"

"Colin!" Janet cried.

"We've got help!" Colin yelled. It was hard to make out what he was saying. "It's – well, you'll see. We're sending him down!"

"What?" said Janet. "What did he say?"

"They're sending someone down," said Alex. "They must have found a farmer or someone. I didn't think they'd had time to get all the way back home."

"Oh, I hope it'll be all right," said Janet anxiously. "I hope they know what they're doing."

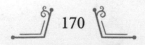

There was the sound of someone coming down the cliff face. They went out on to the ledge. A large shape, black against the snowy cliffs and the darkening sky. It was dark. When had that happened? Not quite night yet, but almost. It would be night by the time they got home. Alex thought of that long journey back through the snow and he shivered.

Whoever was coming down had proper equipment, even Alex could see that. He was properly abseiling down the cliff. Or – no, was he? As he got closer, Alex realised that all he had was a length of rope wrapped round his body and beneath his legs. He was holding the rope behind him and using the friction of his own body to

control his speed. Still, he was moving much faster than Alex and Janet had.

He was a tall, skinny man in a long coat, like someone out of a war film. He looked... There was something familiar about him, though Alex couldn't say what exactly. He looked kind and competent. For the first time since coming to 1947 he felt safe. Like there was someone who knew what they were doing who would look after them.

He turned to Janet and saw that something strange had happened to her. Her face – if possible – had gone even whiter than before. She was staring at the man with her mouth open and her hands clenched into fists.

"What is it?" said Alex. "Janet, what's the

matter? Are you all right?"

The man landed on the ledge beside them with an expert *crunch*.

"Hullo!" he said. "Everything all right here? I don't know, Jan, I leave you for a couple of years, and everything goes to pot…"

"Oh!" Janet cried. "Oh, you've come back! You've come back!"

She flung herself at him and wrapped her arms round his neck. He looked rather taken aback, but he put his arms round her and gathered her up.

"Hey…" he said. "My little girl … my darling girl… Of course I came back. You didn't think I was going to stay on the other side of the world forever, did you?"

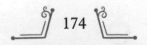

Later. Much later. Hot-water bottles and tea, and a trip up the cliff face with the children's father and his ropes and harnesses. The stumbling journey back to the road – Alex was so tired he thought he might fall asleep on his feet – and then suddenly, miraculously, the arrival of Grandfather and several other men from the village with a Land Rover. And a bath filled up with kettle after saucepan after kettle of hot water, which Alex thought was the most wonderful bath he'd ever had in his life. And hot soup and home-made bread, and cigarettes for the men (the history books at school seemed to have forgotten just how much everyone *smoked* in the past) and the fire in the kitchen blazing full blast, and the tarnished silver locket on the table before them.

"So the treasure's gone," their father said. "Your mother would be sorry. She said it was like something out of *Treasure Island*, all spilling out of leather satchels on to the floor. But I don't know that I mind so very much. Nice to think there's still some buried treasure left in the world."

"The necklace was the treasure really," said Janet contentedly. She was leaning against her father's shoulder, holding his hand as though she'd never let go.

"But it's Mrs Eddington's treasure," said Ruby. "Shouldn't we take it back to her?"

"And find out if she's going to give you your

job back?" said Alex. "Sorry," he added in the children's father's general direction, but he didn't seem that worried. "It's just that we've come this far. We want to know how the story ends."

"And so do I," the children's father said. "You're quite right. We should. And we shall."

CHAPTER TEN
THE CHILD
IN THE PICTURE

Oakden was the village manor house; in modern Dalton it was a hotel. It looked wonderfully grand and mysterious in the snow. *Like a house in a ghost story*, Alex thought. He shivered.

An old man in a black suit – a butler, perhaps?

– opened the door and showed them into the drawing room, where an old woman was sitting by the fire. Although the time for candles was long over, her electric lights were still off and the whole room was lit by candlelight, which gave it a strange, intimate, half-real air.

She looked up as they came into the room. "Well, well," she said. "Look who's home from the wars. Back like a bad penny, are we?"

The children's father crossed the floor and kneeled beside her. "I'm sorry," he said. "Today, more than one thing that was lost is returned." He gave her an envelope.

She looked at him suspiciously, then opened it. Her expression changed. Alex thought perhaps she was going to cry.

"Oh!" she said, and she lifted up the necklace.

It was the first time Alex had seen it in the light, and he was surprised again by how very plain it looked. It was a small, rather simple locket, hanging on a broken silver chain. Alex couldn't see why the old lady had cared so much about losing it.

Mrs Eddington fumbled with the catch – the children's father leant forward to help, but she shook her head – and the locket opened.

Inside was a very old-fashioned black-and-white photograph of a baby. Quite an old baby, old enough to sit up. It was wearing a long, lacy white dress, rather like a christening gown, and its hair was all in curls around its cheeks.

Inside the locket was a tiny lock – *So that's why they're called lockets!* thought Alex, pleased – of faded yellow hair. The old lady lifted it out, and now she did begin to cry, tiny tear tracks running down her soft cheeks.

"Oh!" said Ruby.

"My little Emmeline," said the old lady. "It's the only picture I ever had of her … and her little curls… She died of scarlatina… I thought I'd lost it forever…"

The children made faces of understanding at each other behind her back. Their father put his hand on her shoulder and she rested her head against his arm.

"Do you think it's going to be all right?" Alex whispered to Ruby. "Do you think he's going to get his job back?"

She made an outraged face at him. "What does it matter?" she said. "She's got her picture. That's what counts."

Later again, back at Applecott House, nobody seemed to want to go to bed, though Sheila was nodding and yawning in her father's arms. They sat round the kitchen fire, and they talked and they talked and they talked.

"Warmest room in the house, the kitchen!" said Grandfather. "Everyone knows that! Can't think *why* we were all freezing to death in the

drawing room. It's a national crisis, eh, what?"
But his eyes were smiling. He had opened a dusty-
looking bottle of port for the children's father,
which was apparently a pretty big deal, and he
was standing by the fireplace with his arm round
Granny.

Alex, watching the bright family circle, felt at
once reluctant to leave and filled with a sudden
longing to see his own parents. His own family.
His own time.

He felt Ruby shift beside him. Perhaps she was
feeling something similar.

"We should go," he said.

They went back into the hall. There was the
mirror, and in it there was the twenty-first-

century hallway, with the door wide open and Aunt Joanna's cat Tabitha lying on the step with her belly turned up to the sunlight.

"All right!" said Ruby. She glanced sideways at Alex. "Ready?"

He nodded. Ready.

They stepped forward …

… and landed in a heap on the floor.

For a moment neither moved, then Ruby said, "Heat! Oh, heat! Oh, blessed, blessed central heating! How did people *cope* so long without you?"

"Dunno," said Alex.

It felt rather weird being back here, when all those people were still stuck in 1947 with no

heat and food rations. Except that they weren't, of course. They were probably old now. Or dead. Alex never got used to this part of time travel.

"And cake!" said Ruby. "And biscuits! And pizza! Ooh, I wonder if Aunt Joanna has any cake left? Aunt Joanna! Aunt Joanna!"

She charged into the kitchen, where Aunt Joanna was sitting at the kitchen table doing her accounts.

"Goodness!" she said, looking up. "Ruby Pilgrim, how on earth have you managed to get that nice new school uniform so filthy in the time it takes you to come downstairs? You look like you've been wearing it for days!"

"We have," said Ruby briefly, heading for

the cake tin on the sideboard. "We've been in 1947 for days and days. Well, *a* day, anyway. Oh, chocolate cake! Hallelujah! Aunt Joanna, are you related to some kids called Colin, Janet and Sheila?"

Aunt Joanna watched her with some amusement. "I was," she said. "They were my big cousins. Their mother was my father's sister."

"Was she?" Alex looked at her with interest, trying to work out the connections. "That means their granny and grandfather were *your* granny and grandfather too! I thought your grandfather was Uncle Edmund!"

They'd met Edmund before. In 1912, he'd been a rather cross sort of man, a bit older than Alex and Ruby's dad. Now Alex thought about it, he had looked a little like Colin and Janet's grandfather. They'd had the same squashed sort of face and the same big nose.

"That," said Ruby, "is seriously weird."

"I was born in 1947, you know," Aunt Joanna went on. "Did you meet me?"

"No," said Alex regretfully. "It was very early 1947; you wouldn't have been born yet." Aunt Joanna's birthday was in April. "Aunt Joanna, did you know they still had rationing after the war stopped?"

"Oh yes." Now she was smiling. "I was seven when it ended. Such an awful thing! I used to play at queuing when I was a little girl, instead of shopping."

"*Seven!*" Ruby stared at her in horror through an enormous slice of chocolate cake. "And did you have to turn the electricity off in the middle of the day too?"

"Well, not usually. 1947 – that was the Great Winter, wasn't it? Have you been learning about that in school?"

"No, Aunt Joanna! We were *there*!"

Alex turned away from the familiar, boring argument and went to cut himself some chocolate cake.

Neither he nor Ruby looked back at the mirror in the hall. If they had, they would have seen that the picture had changed. It now showed a sunny day, an open doorway, a still moment that could have belonged to any time at all in the last two hundred years. A bee buzzed lazily past. Hollyhocks bobbed their long heads across the door jamb from the flowerbed outside. And a child wandered through the reflection, head bent over an open book.

Another Pilgrim, another story. Another summer day. Another time.

In all the years the mirror had hung in that house, there had always been children, and gardens, and stories. And so there would be again, *per omnia saecula saeculorum*. Forever and ever amen.

In Aunt Joanna's hallway, all was still. In the

mirror, the child walked across the floor, lost in the book, through the open doorway, and was gone.

TAKE ANOTHER TRIP THROUGH TIME WITH ALEX AND RUBY!

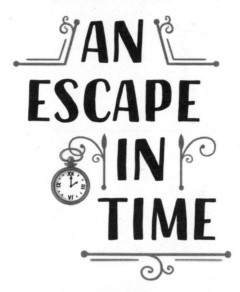

AN ESCAPE IN TIME

CHAPTER ONE
THE APPEARANCE
IN A HALLWAY

In the hallway of Aunt Joanna's house, there was a magic mirror.

Huge, gold-framed and mysterious, there it hung, looking innocent.

Ruby Pilgrim *glared* at it.

"Just look at that!" she said indignantly. "Sitting there like a lump of glass! Like it's just – a reflecting thing or something!"

"It is a reflecting thing," said her brother, Alex. "It's just … sometimes it's a time-travelling thing as well."

Because sometimes the mirror showed another reflection, of another Applecott House in another time. Last summer, they'd gone back to 1912 and helped save a priceless golden cup. Ruby still hadn't sorted out how she felt about that. She'd hated it and she'd loved it, all at the same time. It had been wonderful … and really, really frightening. For quite a lot of it, she'd been certain they were going to be stuck in 1912 forever, and probably have to go and live in a workhouse or something and...

It still made her go cold to remember it.

But then at Christmas they'd come back to Applecott House, and this time they'd stepped back into 1872. They'd landed in a gloriously Victorian Christmas, with plum pudding, and ice skating on the lake, and charades. There'd been danger there too, but most of it had been simply wonderful.

Ruby didn't like to admit it, but she missed it. All this last year, in a busy, noisy secondary school in a little northern town, where the only things anyone seemed to care about was what sort of shoes you wore, and what sort of music you liked, and who fancied who … Ruby had found her thoughts tugging back again and again to that other time, where magic existed and wishes came true and girls her age wore pinafores and petticoats, and didn't have to worry about things like eyeliner and tweezers and shaving their legs. The past, though she would never have said so out loud, had been rather restful.

But now it was half-term. They'd come back to Aunt Joanna's house for their cousin's wedding, and were staying on a couple of days so that their parents could help Aunt Joanna with the repairs to the house. And this time…

This time, she kept looking at the glass, hoping it would change.

"I was so sure it would open again," she said. "But why would it? It's not like we're anyone special really, are we?"

"I suppose not," said Alex sadly.

They both looked back at the mirror.

Which was reflecting another room.

"Oh!" said Ruby.

The room in the mirror was, very definitely, not in Applecott House. It was clearly a much grander place, with blue walls and tall windows showing a large formal garden. There was an elaborate-looking fireplace behind it, with enormous golden candlesticks on the mantel. Ruby didn't have time to properly take this in, though, because all at once a person appeared in the frame.

It was a very, *very* superior-looking person, in a long, loose gown, of the sort that needs an awful lot of artifice to look natural. At least, Ruby supposed it did; the person had a very narrow waist, which *must* mean she was wearing a corset, and her hair, though loose-ish, was *elaborately* loose, with three curls hanging *here*, and a big bouffy bit *here*, and it was a very unnatural-looking greyish-white, as though someone had covered it in powder.

Her cap was complicated too, with lots of lacy bits, and there was more lace round her neck, and ribbons on her sleeves, and what looked like little roses on her shoes. She looked like a very rich person who had spent an hour this morning dressing herself up to look like a very expensive milkmaid.

She appeared to be in a state of panic. She was shouting at someone outside the frame and pulling at them. Alex and Ruby couldn't hear what she said, but she seemed to be pleading with someone just out of sight. She stumbled backwards, and the person was revealed. He was a boy about Ruby's age or a little older, dressed in a blue suit complete with waistcoat, short, tight trousers that came to his knees, white stockings and blue shoes with shiny silver buckles. He had shaggy brown hair that touched his shoulders and he too looked terrified. He was shouting and crying hysterically. His hands flapped in the air in front of him and his mother grabbed them, pulling them down, and then –

And then they stumbled sideways against the mirror.

And vanished.

"Where have they gone?" said Ruby. She scrambled off the window seat. "They should be here! Shouldn't they? Shouldn't they have come here? Where are they?"

"How should I know?" said Alex. Then: "Look!"

Another person had appeared in the mirror. It was a girl who could have been anywhere from about fifteen to nineteen. She was dressed more simply, in a long, plain dress, and her hair, though curled, was less artfully arranged. She ran up to the mirror and her eyes widened in shock. She could see them – Alex was sure of it. She was staring at *him*.

They both, almost without thinking, moved closer to the mirror – so close that they could have reached out and touched the girl if they'd wanted. It was strangely intimate, the three of them there looking so intently at each other, separated only by the glass. Ruby hardly dared to move in case the girl vanished. Who was she? What was happening?